Send in the Clowns!

OTHER YEARLING BOOKS YOU WILL ENJOY:

WRITE UP A STORM WITH THE POLK STREET SCHOOL, *Patricia Reilly Giff*

COUNT YOUR MONEY WITH THE POLK STREET SCHOOL, *Patricia Reilly Giff*

THE POSTCARD PEST, *Patricia Reilly Giff*

TURKEY TROUBLE, *Patricia Reilly Giff*

SHOW TIME AT THE POLK STREET SCHOOL, *Patricia Reilly Giff*

LOOK OUT, WASHINGTON, D.C.!, *Patricia Reilly Giff*

GREEN THUMBS, EVERYONE, *Patricia Reilly Giff*

SECOND-GRADE PIG PALS, *Kirby Larson*

CODY AND QUINN, SITTING IN A TREE, *Kirby Larson*

ANNIE BANANIE AND THE PEOPLE'S COURT, *Leah Komaiko*

Send in
the Clowns!

Judy Delton

Illustrated by Alan Tiegreen

A YEARLING BOOK

Published by
Bantam Doubleday Dell Books for Young Readers
a division of
Random House, Inc.
1540 Broadway
New York, New York 10036

Visit us on the Web! www.randomhouse.com

Educators and librarians, for a variety of teaching tools, visit us at www.randomhouse.com/teachers

ISBN: 0-440-41522-5

Printed in the United States of America

July 1999

10 9 8 7 6 5 4 3

CWO

For Sheila, who adds poetry to my life.

And to brand-new little Harry,
welcome to our family!
Happy birthday, Harry!

Contents

CHAPTER 1

No More Teachers

"We're free! We're free!" shouted Sonny Stone, throwing his notebooks and school papers in the trash can outside the school.

"Well, at least he's neat," said Mary Beth Kelly in disgust. "He didn't just throw his stuff on the lawn like he used to."

"I hate that school's out," said Rachel Meyers. "School's my favorite thing. I like learning new stuff."

Molly Duff was thinking the same thing, but she didn't say it out loud. Kids thought it was uncool to like school. Hey—that rhymed! Uncool to like school! Molly liked to write poems. And she liked to write stories. And lists. She simply liked to write anything.

She also liked to read. She and Mary Beth (who was her best friend) went to the library every week and got lots of books to take home. No, Molly was not glad school was out for the summer. Some kids went on vacations to lakes or mountains, or even on a cruise, like Jody George. His family was rich, and they traveled a lot.

But Molly didn't travel. Her mom and dad both had jobs and didn't get much time off. It would be a long summer.

"We're going to Alaska," said Roger White. "Me and my dad."

"My dad and I," said Rachel.

"You're going to Alaska too?" asked Roger.

Rachel glared at him. "I mean you're supposed to say 'my dad and I.' "

Roger groaned. "Don't try to teach me no English," he said. "I know how to talk."

Rachel rolled her eyes. "That's a double negative," she said. Then she turned to Molly and Mary Beth and said, "I'm glad he's going. He can't go far enough away for me."

Roger was a bully. He made trouble in school and in Pee Wee Scouts. Molly was one of twelve Pee Wee Scouts. They met every Tuesday all year long in Mrs. Peters's basement. The Pee Wees were all seven years old and in second grade. They had a good time together, earning badges and doing good deeds and learning new things. Even with troublemaker Roger, Pee Wee Scouts were fun.

All the Pee Wees seemed to be in the

park. School had let out early because it was the last day. The Pee Wees had some time to kill before their weekly meeting at Mrs. Peters's.

"What are we going to do all summer?" moaned Mary Beth, throwing herself on the grass in the park.

"We can go to the library," said Lisa Ronning.

"We do that anyway," said Mary Beth. "We can't live at the library every day all summer."

Mary Beth was right, Molly thought. Even libraries got boring if you went too often, and if you read all the books Mrs. Nelson would let you take out. Molly and Mary Beth had read almost all the books there.

"There's always Pee Wee Scouts," said Kevin Moe, doing push-ups on the grass.

"Thank goodness for Pee Wees," said Jody, who was in his wheelchair.

Jody and Kevin were both very smart. Molly wanted to marry one of them. She just couldn't make up her mind which one she liked better. If she married Jody, she'd get to ride in his wheelchair anytime she wanted. That was something Kevin could not offer her. But Kevin was going to be mayor someday. Maybe even president. That sounded good too. Molly sighed. At least she had a while to think about it. Her mother said second-graders should not be thinking about boys and dating.

Tracy Barnes sneezed. "I'm allergic to spring," she said into her tissue.

"Hey, you should get a badge for sneezing!" said Roger. He laughed at his own joke. "Nobody can sneeze as good as you!"

Tracy made a face at him. "Allergies

6

aren't funny," she said. "They're an afflic-
tion, my mom says."

"Well, I hope Mrs. Peters has some big
fun project for us," said Mary Beth. "I
wonder what our new badge will be for."

The Pee Wees had just earned a com-
puter badge, a bike safety badge, and a
Wild West badge. It was fun earning those
badges, thought Molly. But this summer's
badge should be the best of all, because
the Scouts had the whole day every day to
work on it.

"Maybe it will be a Pee Wee trip!" said
Tim Noon. "Remember when we went
skiing and got caught in a blizzard? That
was great!"

"We can't get caught in a blizzard," said
Kenny Baker. "It doesn't snow in July."

Kenny was Patty Baker's twin brother.
Sometimes their cousin Ashley Baker from
California would visit, so she was a tem-

porary Scout. Ashley wouldn't be around this summer, though. She would be busy with her Saddle Scouts back home.

"I know it doesn't snow," said Tim. "But that doesn't mean we can't take a trip. We don't have to ski. We could swim or hike or something."

"We already got our swimming badge," Tracy reminded them. "We swam in Jody's pool. He had that great pool party."

All the Pee Wees looked at Jody with admiration. No one else had a pool. Minnesota was not the place for pools. Most of the year it was too cold to use them.

Molly looked at her watch. "Rat's knees!" she said. "It's almost time for our meeting! We're going to be late!"

The Scouts jumped up and started for Mrs. Peters's house. No one wanted to be late. Scout meetings meant surprises. No one ever knew what that next badge would be! Or what they would have to do to get it!

CHAPTER 2

The Perfect Badge

"Guess what?" called Mrs. Peters from her front door when she saw the Pee Wees arrive. "The circus is coming to town for one exciting night."

The Pee Wees were excited. The circus could make the summer fun. But what did it have to do with the Pee Wee Scouts and earning a badge?

The Pee Wees scampered down the basement steps. Sonny's mother, Mrs. Stone, who was assistant Scout leader, followed them with a plate of cupcakes.

"I'm glad that got your attention," their leader said, "because the circus has something to do with our new badge!"

"Yay!" shouted all the Pee Wees.

Sometimes when Mrs. Peters talked about a new badge, it didn't sound like much fun. Like going to a nursing home, or learning bike rules. In the end things always turned out all right, but Molly liked a badge to sound good right from the start. None of the Pee Wees liked Mrs. Peters to announce badges with words like *learning*, *working*, *helping*, and *project*. That was too much like school, and Pee Wees were supposed to have fun. They wanted badges described with words like *play*, *circus*, *picnic*, *ball game*, *travel*, *farm*, and *swimming*.

"Do we get a badge just for going to the circus, Mrs. Peters?" Kenny asked.

"For eating cotton candy?" Patty asked.

"Maybe for riding on the Ferris wheel," Lisa said.

"You're close," laughed Mrs. Peters. "But you'll have to do a little more work than that!"

Now the Pee Wees groaned.

"This year," said their leader when they had settled down, "we have been asked to participate in the circus!"

"You mean like ride on an elephant?" asked Tracy. "I'm allergic to elephants."

"I could dance in the center ring," said Rachel. "I take ballet, you know."

"Hey, I could do a high-wire act," said Roger. "I could ride my bike on one of those ropes they string up!"

Mrs. Peters smiled. "You may get a chance to do some of those things," she said. "The circus coming here is not a big one. It's a small group that goes to different towns to raise money for charity. They like for local residents to take part. Our Scout troop has been asked to help out! So we can not only have fun but earn money for charity at the same time!"

Molly's mind was spinning. What could she do in a circus? She was afraid of high places. She certainly couldn't be a trapeze artist on one of those swings way above the crowd. She didn't want to fall to the ground, or even into a net.

And wild animals were dangerous! What if she had a small-dog act and got stepped on by an elephant or eaten by a lion?

"I think I'd rather watch a circus than be in one," Molly told Mary Beth.

"Being in it might be fun," said her friend.

"I want to be a clown!" shouted Sonny, making a funny face and pretending to have big floppy feet.

"You *are* a clown," Rachel said in disgust.

Sonny began doing cartwheels around the room.

"I wouldn't mind selling cotton candy," said Patty.

"Do we get paid for being in the circus?" asked Lisa.

"No," Mrs. Peters answered. "Remember, this is charity work. We do it to help and to have fun. I'll list some of the things the Pee Wees can do on the blackboard. Then you can think about them while we have our cupcakes, and sign up for the one you choose before we leave today."

Mrs. Peters picked up a piece of chalk and began to write.

1. *Ticket taker*
2. *Animal feeder*
3. *Cleaner upper*

4. *Trapeze artist*
5. *Elephant rider*
6. *Clown*
7. *Unicycle performer*
8. *Magician*
9. *Dog trainer*
10. *Dancer*

"You won't have to do these things alone," Mrs. Peters said. "There will be people to teach you things like how to be a funny clown. And how to ride a unicycle. They'll be nearby to make sure you don't get hurt."

"Hey, I don't need help," shouted Sonny. "I can ride a unicycle by myself. That's what I want to do in the circus!"

"Ha," said Roger. "You've still got training wheels on your bike! How are you going to ride on only one wheel that's way up in the air?"

1. TICKET TAKER
2. ANIMAL FEEDER
3 CLEANER UPPER
4 TRAPEZE ARTIST
5 ELEPHANT RIDER
6 CLOWN.
7. UNICYCLE
8. MAGICIA
9. DOG TRA
10. DANC

"I can," said Sonny, getting red in the face. "I'll show you!"

"I want to dance!" Rachel said, twirling around on her toes. "And I don't need any help with that either. I'm a born dancer, my teacher says so."

Mrs. Peters held up her hand. "Let's give this some thought," she said, "so you can choose the right thing. Maybe you'll think of something else you want to do, too.

Most of the Pee Wees already had decided what they wanted to do. They gobbled down their cupcakes and ran to sign up.

Molly had no idea what she wanted to do in the circus. She wasn't even sure she wanted to go to the circus. She remembered that when she went to one with her dad, a pony had stepped on her shoe, and she had gotten sick on one of the rides. It was dangerous enough to *go* to a circus, she thought, let alone to *be* in one.

"I want to be one of those ladies who wears a sparkling dress and stands on a horse's back as the horse runs around the ring," said Lisa. "Can I do that, Mrs. Peters?"

"Some things may be too dangerous," said their leader.

"That's not as dangerous as being on a trapeze," said Lisa.

"A trapeze has a net under it," Mrs. Peters said. "So if you fall you can't get hurt."

"What if I rode a horse bareback, but sitting down?"

"That sounds more likely," said their leader.

Molly looked the list over. There was nothing that wasn't scary! Even with a net! Unless of course, she took tickets at the door. But what fun was that? Even feeding the animals could give a lion a chance to bite off her arm!

"I'm going to sign up for cleanup," said Kenny. "I like to clean our garage. I'm good at that."

"What are you going to do?" Mary Beth asked her best friend.

Molly shook her head. "I don't know," she sighed. "I thought a circus badge would be fun, but this feels scary."

"You could dance," said Mary Beth. "That isn't scary."

"I don't know how to dance!" said Molly. "Anyway, Rachel is choosing that."

"Mrs. Peters said we'll get help. I think the circus people will teach you," said her friend.

Even with help, Molly didn't think she could learn to be good enough to dance in a circus ring. In front of strangers. Lots of strangers. Crowds of people who had come to the circus to be entertained!

"I'm going to do a high-wire act!" said Roger. "I'm going to ride my bike way up in the air!"

All the Pee Wees remembered when Roger rode his bike backward down the playground slide and had to go to the hospital. Molly and Mary Beth had saved his life by dialing 911. It sounded to Molly as if Roger hadn't learned his lesson.

"No one is going to save you this time if you fall with your bike," said Rachel.

Roger made a face. "I won't fall."

By the time the Pee Wees had told what good deeds they had done, and sung their Pee Wee song, and said their Pee Wee pledge, all the Pee Wees except Molly had signed up. She read the list.

Roger on the high wire.

Kenny in cleanup.

Rachel to dance.

Lisa as a bareback horse rider.

Sonny on a unicycle.

Tim as ticket taker. He must be scared too, Molly thought. Now everything left was really scary!

Jody to feed the animals.

Tracy to be a clown.

Kevin to have a dog act.

Patty and Mary Beth to ride on an elephant.

It looked as if the only thing left for Molly was to be a magician! And Molly had no idea how to do magic!

CHAPTER **3**

Molly the Magician

"**Y**ou should have signed up with me to ride on the elephant," said Mary Beth.

"I'm afraid of elephants," said Molly. "They're so . . . big."

"Well, now you have to pull rabbits out of a hat, and how can you do that?" Mary Beth asked. "Patty and I will just sit on an elephant and ride. Anyone could do it."

"Anyone who isn't afraid of heights," said Molly.

But Mary Beth was right. It would be

23

easier to ride an elephant than to do magic when you had no idea how.

How to pull a rabbit from a hat.

How to pull scarves from your sleeve.

How to saw a person in half.

"What's the worst that could happen?" Rachel said to Molly. "You'll just look silly if your tricks don't work."

Was Rachel right? Was Molly worrying for nothing?

"But it would be embarrassing not to do it right," said Mary Beth. "Everyone would boo you. 'Boo, boo, boo,' they'd say. You'd turn red and no one would clap when you finished. Outside of that . . ."

"It's just your reputation you have to worry about," said Tracy. "At least you'll be on the ground and not up in the air on an elephant or on a high wire."

Mary Beth and Tracy were right. Failing

24

BILLINGS COUNTY PUBLIC SCHOOL
Box 307
Medora, North Dakota 58645

was scary. And embarrassing. Whether it was in school or in the circus. Magic was definitely not the best thing to have chosen. But it was better than doing something high in the air.

Mrs. Peters clapped her hands. "The circus arrives next Saturday morning," she said. "They'll set their tents up in the park, and unload their animals and equipment from the trucks at about ten o'clock. Let's all be there to meet them, and start practicing! Our performance will be Saturday afternoon, so be prepared.

"Meanwhile, think about what you would like to wear. We'll have to show up in our own costumes, so get busy! See you all Saturday in the park!"

Rat's knees! Molly definitely had a lot of work to do before Saturday! She had to find out about magic. And practice it. How could she pull rabbits out of hats with no practice? And where did the rabbit come from? Did it really appear out of nowhere by magic? Was magic real?

Mary Beth would not have to practice riding an elephant. Not once.

Rachel would not have to practice dancing. She knew how.

Even Jody wouldn't have to practice feeding the animals. The circus keeper would give him food and he would give it to the animals. Molly should be feeding animals. She fed her own dog at home with no trouble. Even having her arm bitten off wasn't as scary right now as doing magic in the center ring!

"I just take tickets at the door," Tim said to Molly as they walked out of Mrs. Peters's house. "Simple."

Tim had it made! He wouldn't even have to think to do his job. He could collect tickets in his sleep!

And give Kenny a broom and he could sweep. Big deal. No one had to practice cleaning.

Molly walked home and wondered if she should talk to her parents about her problem. But she hated to go whining like a baby and asking for help. She was in second grade.

"Don't bite off more than you can chew," her grandma always told her.

Her mother and dad were tired after work and often said they liked to come home and relax. They don't need to worry about how I'll learn magic in a few days! Molly thought. This is my problem, and I have to solve it.

All week long the Pee Wees talked about what they were going to wear and how much fun they would have being in the circus. All the Pee Wees, that is, except for Molly. She was so worried about what she would do once she got into that ring, she didn't even think about a costume. Mrs. Peters said the circus people would help, but what if they didn't? What if the time came and Molly was left on her own with no magic at all?

One night Kevin called her to ask to borrow a dog leash.

"I've got these dogs to practice my small-dog act with," he said. "They can do three tricks already!"

Tracy called to tell her she was taking clown lessons at the clown club.

"I learned how to paint my face with a big red nose and blue cheeks," she said. "I get to squirt water out of a flower on my shirt and throw candy to the kids."

Anyone could do those things, thought Molly. But I still don't know what I'm going to do.

When her dad came in to use the phone,

he said, "How are those circus plans coming?"

"Fine," lied Molly.

"Need any help?" he asked.

"No," Molly lied again. She could see that her dad had other things on his mind. Important things. She would solve this herself. The library was a good place to look for help.

"Here's a book called *Magic Made Easy*," said Mrs. Nelson, the librarian. That was exactly what Molly needed! She took the book and sat down in a quiet corner to read it. It told about lots of magic tricks, but they all seemed really hard. Molly finally decided that three of them sounded pretty easy. She chose picking a rabbit out of a hat. And pulling scarves out of her sleeve. And throwing her voice, which was also known as ventriloquism. Molly had seen ventriloquists on TV. They always had a dummy on their knee and made it talk. How hard could that be?

The next morning Molly packed a big bag of stuff and went to Mary Beth's to practice.

"It says here you have to get a big red scarf, and a fake thumb," said Mary Beth. "Before you go onstage, you fold the scarf up real small and stick it into the thumb. Then you put the fake thumb on your real thumb. When you're in front of a crowd, you snap off the fake thumb real fast and the scarf comes out like magic."

Molly had a red wool winter scarf. But it was too thick to fit in a thumb. "Where do I get an artificial thumb anyway?" she asked.

"I guess at a magic shop," said her friend. "If you have enough money."

Molly shook her head. "I don't. I just bought my aunt's birthday present."

Mary Beth thought for a moment. "I suppose we could make one out of some old rubber gloves," she said. "My mom threw some out. They're in the garage."

The girls ran and got the gloves. They were perfect! Molly cut the thumb off one of them and put it on her thumb. It was too big.

"It won't be once the scarf is stuffed in it," said Mary Beth. "Even your thick red scarf will fit. We won't have to get a new one."

The girls stuffed the scarf into the thumb. It stretched and got huge. When Molly put it on her thumb, it looked as if she had a boxing glove on!

"It's the best you can do," said Mary Beth. "Now snap it off real fast and pull out the scarf."

Molly gave it a try. She tugged her thumb. It didn't snap. And when she fi-

nally did pull it off, the scarf stayed inside. By the time she pulled it out and waved it around, her trick didn't look like magic. It looked like Molly taking a heavy scarf out of a balloon.

"You'll just have to practice until you can do it faster," Mary Beth said. "There's no other way. We'd better get to the next trick. You have a lot to learn."

Molly pulled an old blue golf hat of her dad's out of her bag for the rabbit trick.

"Aren't you supposed to use a big black hat?" asked Mary Beth.

"This is all I've got," Molly said. "It will have to work."

This whole magic thing is so hard, thought Molly. Big deal if my hat isn't perfect. It's good enough for me, and the rabbit won't know the difference between a blue hat and a black one. She'd be fine. Her trick would be okay because she would practice as much as she had to. That was all she needed to earn her badge—a little practice. And she could do that, no problem.

"Hey, Molly," Mary Beth said. "Where are you going to get a rabbit?"

CHAPTER 4

Magic Is Not Easy

"Oh no," Molly said. "I don't know how I'll find a rabbit."

"I think Roger has a rabbit," said Mary Beth.

"We can't use Roger's rabbit," said Molly. "Roger hates us."

Mary Beth stamped her foot. "We can't be fussy," she said. "We need a rabbit and he's got one."

The girls walked over to Roger's house.

"May we borrow your rabbit?" asked

Molly politely when he answered the door.

"Go away," said Roger, slamming the door.

Molly could see Roger through an open window. He was eating cornflakes.

"We'll pay you," Mary Beth yelled through the window.

Roger reopened the door. "How much?"

"Well, I don't have any money," said Molly.

"She'll let you be in her act," Mary Beth volunteered.

"What can I do?" asked Roger suspiciously.

"You can be the dummy in the ventriloquist act," said Mary Beth quickly.

Rat's knees, thought Molly. She didn't want to hold Roger on her knee!

"No way," said Roger. "I'm no dummy."

Mary Beth stuck her foot in the door. "You can be the ventriloquist," she said. "Molly will be the dummy."

What had Mary Beth just said? Molly was *not* going to sit on Roger's knee!

Roger was thinking as he ate a Pop-Tart. "Okay," he finally said. "I'll lend you my rabbit. But you have to be nice to Fluffy."

"We will," Molly promised.

"We're just going to pull her out of a hat. We won't even need her until show time. Just bring her to the circus for the performance. And get ready to do the ventriloquist trick. You and Molly can practice tomorrow."

"I'm not going to practice that. I'll be ready on Saturday. Bye." Roger slammed the door.

"That settles everything," Mary Beth said. She seemed very pleased.

On the way home, Molly said, "I thought a dummy was a big doll with a mouth that opens and shuts."

"You can do that," said Mary Beth. "Roger won't be the dummy. And you need his rabbit. Anyway, now you don't have to find a real dummy."

"I guess," Molly said. "I'd better hurry home and practice."

"Well," Mary Beth said, "we told Roger you won't use Fluffy until show time. And I doubt you really want to practice the ventriloquist act with him. You'll just have to wing it."

"How will I do that?" shrieked Molly.

"Just read your book and figure out the rabbit trick. It shouldn't be too hard. And a dummy doesn't really say anything," said Mary Beth. "Roger is supposed to throw his voice and pull a string to open and shut your mouth."

Molly stared at her. "There is no string on my neck," she said. "And I'll bet Roger has no idea how to throw his voice."

"It will work out," said Mary Beth. "You'll see. Just practice the scarf act and I'm sure the rabbit thing and the dummy thing will be okay. I've got to go home. My grandma's coming to take me shopping."

Mary Beth waved and walked away humming, just as happy as could be. Rat's knees! It dawned on Molly that her best friend, and all the rest of the Pee Wees too, were not worried about their circus acts the way she was. They didn't worry about *anything* the way she did!

Molly practiced the scarf act, and it did not go well. The scarf simply did not pop out of the rubber thumb very fast. She had to tug it out. That didn't seem very magical. The audience would see through the trick in a flash.

Well, at least she had a rabbit. And a dummy! (Even though *she* was the dummy!) She would cross her fingers and hope the circus people would help her figure the rest out. She only had one more day to wait because tomorrow was Saturday and the circus was coming!

In the morning, all the Pee Wees were at the park bright and early. The Peterses were there, and most of the parents.

Sonny was pushing his unicycle, but Molly noticed he was not riding it. Tracy had on her clown outfit. She had big floppy orange shoes and an orange wig. Rachel was dressed in her tutu and was standing on her toes, even though it wasn't time for her act.

"Rachel is showing off," Lisa whispered. "She doesn't need that tutu yet. She just likes an excuse to look like a dancer."

What Lisa said was probably true. But Molly had to admit that if she could dance she would want to wear a tutu too. It took a lot of lessons and hard work to be a dancer.

As the Pee Wees and the crowd watched, the big circus trucks pulled up to the park and began to unload. The Pee Wees cheered. Roger whistled and Sonny and the other boys stamped their feet and shouted.

"Hooray for the circus!" shouted Jody.

"On with the show!" Kenny yelled. "We want elephants! We want elephants!"

The rest of the crowd picked up the

42

cheer and chanted it over and over. A circus man with a big mermaid tattoo on his arm put a ramp in place behind a big truck. Then he opened the truck's back door.

Down the ramp came a reluctant elephant.

Just one elephant.

A small elephant. A shy elephant.

"It's not very big," said Tracy.

Now Molly really wished she had signed up to ride on it. A small elephant. And it seemed like an old, slow, friendly elephant. Not one that would run off with people on its back.

The man with the tattoo led the elephant down the ramp and tied it to a pole.

"I don't think they need to tie it," said Rachel. "It's not going anywhere. It looks like it needs a nap."

There were not many other animals—

just a few dogs with fluffy balls on their tails and blue ribbons tied on their ears.

"There's my horse!" shouted Lisa. "The one I'll ride bareback! Look how pretty she is!"

This is not a big circus, Molly thought. The horse was not big. The elephant was not big. The dogs were not big. Even the tents were not big. The trapeze was so low you didn't need a ladder to get to it.

The circus people were very friendly. They shook the Pee Wees' hands and said how glad they were to be there. And the crowd cheered the small circus just as though it were the biggest, tallest, most amazing circus ever.

"I'm Max," the elephant trainer told the Pee Wees. "You all look like good helpers. And there are so many of you! What a great time we'll have!"

Will I have a great time? Molly wondered. It all depended on a red scarf, Roger's rabbit, and what kind of a dummy she could be! One thing for sure, she would soon find out.

CHAPTER 5

Let the Games Begin!

"It took a long time to set up the circus," Kenny said when the Pee Wees came back from a late lunch. The crowds were arriving. "But it looks like they're ready to go already! I guess the circus people aren't going to practice with us now."

The circus people were very busy indeed. Families were lining up to buy tickets from Max, who seemed to do a lot of jobs under the big top. He took people's money, then handed them tickets. The people handed their tickets to Tim and sat on one of the folding chairs a circus clown was setting up. The clown had a red nose, but otherwise he looked like anyone else. He wore regular clothes. Tracy definitely looked more like a clown than the real one did!

Molly started to get nervous. If the circus started soon, she'd have to do her magic act without any more practice. No one from the circus had helped her yet. She saw Roger and tried to ask him if he was ready to do the dummy act and if Fluffy was around, but he didn't pay attention to her. It looked as if he was arguing with his mom. They both kept pointing to his bike.

"He's probably ready," Molly told herself. "Don't worry so much."

Some of the children walked over and patted the elephant on its trunk. And others watched the horse paw the ground. The clown threw the kids some candy.

"That must be where the circus people sleep," said Lisa, pointing to a trailer parked nearby.

"It's probably where they put on their costumes and stuff too," said Tracy.

But when the entertainers came out of the trailer, they weren't wearing costumes. They were wearing blue jeans and T-shirts.

"I think we're overdressed," said Rachel, looking at Lisa in her bareback riding costume. And Tracy stood out with her bright orange wig.

"Maybe they'll put on their costumes later," said Jody.

But later there still were no costumes. Instead, Max walked over to the low trapeze in his blue jeans. He put his leg over it and began to swing. The crowd cheered.

The swing went back and forth, not very high, and then the clown with the red nose jumped on beside him. The crowd went wild. They both did a somersault off the swing and landed on their feet on the grass.

"My little brother can do that and he's only four," scoffed Mary Beth.

Max and the clown were bowing. People were clapping and clapping. One lady even threw flowers at their feet!

Max held up his hand for silence. "I believe one of our Tee Bee Scouts is going to help us on the high wire," he said, looking around the tent.

"Not Tee Bee!" shouted Kevin. "We're *Pee Wee* Scouts!"

"I'm sorry," said Max. "I meant the Sea Bee Scouts!"

Kevin groaned.

"It's an easy mistake," said Mrs. Peters.

"The circus people are not familiar with our Scout troop."

"What little Sea Bee is going to join us in this dangerous high-wire act?" asked Max.

Roger held up both hands. He ran toward the swing, waving to the audience. He was wearing gym clothes and a helmet.

Max held Roger's hand up and they both bowed.

"I see the Sea Bees come prepared!" said Max. "It's good to protect your head while performing such a dangerous high-wire feat."

"Where is the high wire?" asked Patty. "I don't see any high wire."

"I think that's it," said Jody, pointing to a rope stretched between two poles and about a foot off the ground.

"Where's his bike?"

"I think Roger's mom said he couldn't ride it on the high wire or he'd be in big trouble. She thought it sounded too dangerous."

I thought it was too dangerous too, Molly thought. But what's so dangerous about walking one foot above the grass?

"If he falls off that," shrieked Kevin, "he'll just land on his feet on the grass! Big deal!"

Max held his hand up again. "I must ask for complete silence during this act. Any sudden noise or movement could cause a serious accident."

The crowd heeded his words. They watched silently as Roger carefully put one foot ahead of the other and tried to walk across the rope. He put his arms out for balance.

"I thought he was going to ride his bike

on a high wire," said Patty. "I mean a *really* high wire!"

Everything was hushed as Roger leaned from one side to the other, trying to keep his balance. He took a few steps—and slipped off. Kevin was right. Roger's feet landed on the grass.

"He sure didn't need a helmet," said Kenny.

Roger tried again. He almost lost his balance a few times, waving his hands in the air. Finally he walked the last few feet along the rope, jumped off, and bowed deeply. He'd made it all the way across.

Now the crowd let loose. They whistled and shouted and clapped.

"What a star!" Max shouted as he slapped Roger on the back. "Well done. Don't you agree, audience?"

They did agree. They cheered all over again. They loved Roger.

Rachel rolled her eyes.

"All I can say is you really chose the wrong act," Mary Beth said to Molly. "You could have done that easy."

Didn't Mary Beth know Molly was thinking the same thing? Why did she have to rub it in?

"After all that excitement," said Max, "we'll take a short break to water the animals. When we come back, another one of our own Sea Bee scouts will give us a great unicycle performance!"

Everyone looked at Sonny. He turned red.

Meanwhile, Kenny went around the tent cleaning up ticket stubs and candy wrappers. Jody wheeled over to the water faucet in the park and filled water dishes for the elephant, the horse, and the dogs. Tim was still taking tickets.

"I surely didn't expect so many people," said Mr. Peters.

"I didn't expect the acts to go so quickly," said Mrs. Peters. "I wonder if there will be enough acts to fill the time!"

"We can do them all over again," said Roger. "I can do an encore anytime!"

During the break, Sonny practiced on his unicycle.

"That's the smallest unicycle I ever saw," said Rachel. "Sonny can reach out and put his feet on the ground if he loses his balance."

But Sonny was not doing well. As soon as he got on and began to pedal, the bike fell over. It landed on top of him.

"Rat's knees, didn't he practice?" muttered Molly.

Sonny's dad tried to help out. He ran

along, holding the bike up. But as soon as he let go, Sonny toppled over.

"I'll bet his dad has to hold him up during the act," said Lisa. "What do you think?"

But suddenly Sonny and his dad left the park with the cycle.

"Where are they going?" asked Roger. "He's on next!"

"He's probably scared," said Rachel. "I would be if I were him. He's going to make a fool of himself on that thing. I'll bet he's running away."

"There's supposed to be a helper," said Kevin. "The circus people are supposed to teach us this stuff."

But when Max walked by with a can of soda, he said he had no idea how to ride a unicycle. "That's too hard for me," he said. "My specialty is the trapeze act."

"The break is almost over," said Mary Beth. "Where is Sonny?"

Even Mrs. Peters looked worried. Maybe he did run away, thought Molly.

Finally two women started making music with some homemade instruments that looked like large cooking pots. Another woman beat a drum to indicate that things were going to start again. The break was over.

But where in the world was the next act?

CHAPTER 6

"In the Center Ring . . ."

Max must not have noticed that Sonny was missing, because he announced in a loud voice that in the center ring (the only ring) Sea Bee Sonny Stoke would ride his unicycle.

The Pee Wees giggled. "Sonny Stoke!" roared Roger. "Hey, where's Sonny Stoke? Stoke the bloke!"

Just as Max finished the introduction, Sonny arrived on his unicycle—alone.

Molly saw that his father was seated in the front row of the audience.

Sonny was riding into the center ring without falling off!

The Pee Wees stared.

"I don't believe it," said Kevin.

The Pee Wees were all surprised to see Sonny on the unicycle, but not because he had finally learned to ride it successfully.

"Rat's knees!" Molly shouted to Mary Beth. "Sonny has training wheels!"

"So that's what Sonny and his dad were doing," said Jody. "That's pretty smart!"

Leave it to Jody to say something positive, thought Molly. Jody always saw the good side of everything.

All the other Pee Wees were booing and laughing at Sonny.

"Hey, Stoke, you bloke!" Roger yelled. "I'll bet you'll put training wheels on your *car* when you get one!"

"What a baby," said Rachel in disgust.

Sonny rode around and around the ring. He raised one hand in the air and waved at the audience. There was no way he could fall over because there were two small wheels on each side of the big wheel.

"He could ride that thing in his sleep," said Tracy.

"Anyone could ride it, even a baby," said Lisa.

When Sonny had ridden around many times, he turned and rode the other way. He rode down the aisle waving to the audience and smiling. Then he rode out the door of the tent. His act was over.

People were laughing, but they were also clapping and cheering. Sonny was a hit. Sonny was a star. The audience loved him. They seemed to like all the acts so far! Molly hoped they would like her too.

Molly wanted to go next. She hoped Max would call her name. First she would do her scarf act, then the rabbit act, and last of all she would have to sit on Roger's knee and be the ventriloquist's dummy. Roger had better be ready, Molly thought. He was a big part of her act. That made her a little nervous.

But Max didn't call Molly's name. He called Rachel's.

Rachel was ready to dance. Recorded music began playing. Rachel glided into the center ring. She didn't make any mistakes. At least, thought Molly, no mistakes anyone could see.

Rachel looked wonderful. She whirled and twirled and stood on her toes and leaped across the ring gracefully. At the end she bowed in a big sweeping curtsey all the way to the floor. The audience did not laugh. They did not boo. They clapped and clapped and asked for an encore.

Rachel did two more dances and bowed again. Someone in the back threw a big bouquet of flowers into the ring.

Rat's knees, thought Molly, Rachel is the only one who didn't goof up at all. She's a real dancer!

"Wow!" said Mary Beth. "She's good. She's really good!"

Well, thought Molly, if Mary Beth or I had taken dance lessons since nursery school, we'd be good too. Or maybe we wouldn't. Maybe Rachel had real talent. Maybe she was a real star!

"I think the Pee Wees are doing all the work," grumbled Kenny. "How come none of the circus guys are doing anything?"

As if someone had heard him, a few performers came out and told jokes. Then one of them danced, but not as well as Rachel. And one rode a unicycle and fell off. The Pee Wees were definitely the best act in town so far. Even with their mistakes!

After another short break for refreshments, Max announced the next act.

"In the center ring," he called, "we have Kevin Moe and his talented dog act!"

"I wonder who's talented," whispered Mary Beth. "Kevin or the dogs!"

Kevin ran into the ring, waving like a real performer. Three little dogs sat on stools, with white collars around their necks. First Kevin said "Speak" and the three dogs barked. Everyone applauded.

"Lucky can do that, and he's not even a show dog," said Lisa. Lucky was Mrs.

Peters's dog. He was the Pee Wee mascot.

Next Kevin held up a hoop in front of the dogs. One by one they sailed through it.

"That's pretty good," said Kenny.

Molly knew Kevin would be good at whatever he chose. He never made a fool of himself the way Sonny did. As she watched his act, Molly decided Kevin was the one she wanted to marry. She was sure Jody was good at feeding the animals and other things, but Kevin had star quality. His act moved along quickly, and the dogs did not run off and hide, or leave the tent, or do anything else embarrassing.

I wonder how he learned to do the tricks, Molly thought. Someone from the circus must have given Kevin a lesson. I hope they come help me make sure my magic works!

"Play dead!" Kevin shouted as his act continued, and the three dogs fell to the ground and did not move. The audience cheered.

Kevin gave another command. The dogs rolled over. They walked on three legs. They did lots of neat tricks. At the end Kevin gave them some dog candy as a reward.

Kevin left the center ring with the dogs, and Molly's knees began to shake. There were four Pee Wee acts left. Bareback riding by Lisa, clowning by Tracy, Mary Beth and Patty on the elephant, and Molly with her magic.

Would the next name Max announced be hers?

CHAPTER 7

Closer and
Closer and . . .

Max walked to the center of the ring and held up his hand for silence. He was going to announce the next act! Molly knew her name would be called. She looked around for Roger. He had promised Fluffy would be ready.

But when Molly saw Roger, he didn't look ready to perform and Fluffy was nowhere to be seen. Roger was trying to get Tracy's orange wig off. He chased her around and around the seats. Finally he decided to bother Sonny instead. How could Molly have trusted Roger to help with her act? She'd had no choice, that was how. She had been desperate for that rabbit!

Max opened his mouth to announce the next act. Molly held her breath until he said, "Lisa Ronning will now do a bare-back act on our dancing pony, Rochelle."

Rochelle did not look happy. Rochelle did not look as if she wanted to dance. Rochelle was the size of a dog.

And her back was not bare. She had a saddle on. Lisa tried to stand up on the saddle, but she slipped off. Finally Max and one of the clowns held her so she wouldn't fall. The dancing pony walked very, very slowly around the ring while Lisa wobbled back and forth on top. But she didn't fall. She smiled and held on to

Max and the clown. Music played, and the act was over.

"I'll bet you're next," said Mary Beth.

"I'll bet *you* are," said Molly crossly. She was tired of waiting to perform. It was like waiting to get a shot in the doctor's office. It got worse and worse the more time there was to think about it.

Molly could see the elephant being led into the ring.

"You're right!" said Mary Beth. "I can't wait!"

Imagine being anxious to do your act, thought Molly.

"Mary Beth Kelly and Patty Baker will now ride atop a giant elephant!" called Max. Then he lowered his voice. "Because of the danger in this act, we ask you once again, audience, to hold your applause until the end. Any sudden noises and the elephant could bolt, causing a nasty accident."

Could the elephant really bolt, thought Molly? Or was Max exaggerating? The animal looked as tired as the pony in Lisa's act. And Mary Beth didn't look worried.

"Hey, is the elephant going to lift them up with its trunk?" Tim asked. "I saw a circus on television and that's how the riders got on top!"

"They don't need much help getting up there," scoffed Kenny. "They could just put their legs over its back if they stood on a little stool."

But nothing was that simple in this circus. The band played a drumroll and each girl was hoisted up to the little basket on the elephant's back by two strong circus workers.

"Wow, is this ever high!" Patty called out.

"We'll be right beside you at all times," said a worker. "You have nothing to fear."

Around and around the ring they went. Plod plod plod. It took a long time. Mary Beth smiled and giggled. But Molly was bored. If the elephant had bolted, at least it would have been exciting. But it didn't. Plod plod plod. Boring boring boring.

My act won't be boring, Molly thought. She herself didn't even know exactly what would happen! But if Max didn't announce her next, she would scream. She and Tracy were the only two Pee Wees left.

The applause for the elephant ride was thunderous. It was so loud, even the elephant looked excited. It lowered its two front legs, and the girls slid down its trunk. Molly thought that was the best part of the act.

Mary Beth walked over to Molly and

said, "That was really scary! I could see everybody in the tent from up there!"

"You looked like you had lots of fun," Molly said.

"I hope I'm next," said Tracy.

Mrs. Peters came over and put her arms around Tracy and Molly.

"I know it's been a long wait," she said, looking at her watch. "I wonder if we will have time to get both acts in."

The circus clowns were pretending to throw buckets of water at the audience, but the buckets were really filled with confetti. People screamed, and then laughed when they saw they weren't getting wet.

Max motioned to Tracy to come and join them!

"She's the only clown in a real costume," Rachel said. She had changed from her dance outfit and now had on jeans and a white blouse. Molly wished her act was over and she could be that relaxed.

Tracy began throwing pails of confetti with the other clowns and squirting water from the fake flower on her shirt. Her large shoes flopped and her baggy pants went up and down on their elastic suspenders. She was very funny and the crowd liked her.

Well, at least Molly was sure of one thing. She would be next. Hers was the only act left!

She put on the magician's cape her mother had made for her, and picked up her bag with the hat and the scarf and the fake thumb in it. She started to walk forward as Tracy left the ring and all the other clowns ran out of the tent.

But just as she got to the ring, Max stood up and said, "And that's it, folks! Let's hand it to those little Sea Bees for all their hard work and good showmanship! Thanks for coming, and please fold your chair and set it by the door on your way out. Every little bit of help is appreciated! Good-bye and see you next year!"

Max threw the audience a kiss, and the people rose to leave.

CHAPTER 8

Better Late Than Never?

Molly stood in her cape and stared. People were leaving. Her parents were having a conversation with the Stones. Mrs. Peters was frowning. Mary Beth looked puzzled.

And then Jody wheeled his chair quickly up to the ring. "Max!" he called. "There's another act! You forgot Molly Duff!"

By now Molly didn't know whether to

be glad she did not have to go on or sorry she was left out. It was both a relief and a disappointment!

When Max heard the news, he stood on one of the stools from the dog act and rang a cowbell that was on a nearby table.

"Hear! Hear!" he cried. "We've made a mistake! We have one more act, folks, Miss Molly Duff!"

But most of the people had filed out, and even the cowbell did not silence the few that were left.

"I'm afraid you'll have to come back to-morrow. We'll do another show before we leave," said Max. "You can be the first act, all fresh and bright. The crowd will enjoy it much more than at the end of a day. It's getting late and everyone is hungry now."

"But how will we get people to come back?" asked Mrs. Peters.

"We'll announce it on the radio to-night," said Max. "On the ten o'clock news."

On the way home, Mary Beth said, "I think the announcement should be on TV. Who listens to the radio news?"

"My grandma does," said Molly. "But she doesn't live here, and she's not coming to the circus."

That night the Pee Wees all were allowed to stay up to hear the announcement on the radio.

"And the weather should be a bit stormy tomorrow," the weatherman said, "so take those umbrellas. Better yet, stay home where it's dry!"

"Well, that's not the thing to tell people!" said Mr. Duff.

"Oh, this announcement is just in," said the news reader. "Before leaving town tomorrow morning, the circus will have one final act at ten o'clock. Max Appel urges you to go. No additional ticket is needed if you attended the circus today. And now I'll say good night, and good news!"

"Well, that should get them there!" said Molly's mother, turning off the radio. She started getting ready for bed.

Get them there? thought Molly. Most people probably had switched their radios off before they heard. Like Molly's act, the announcement was almost forgotten! And the advice to stay home during the rain wasn't helpful either.

But if no one came, Molly wouldn't have to do her act! That would be great.

But if she didn't do her act, she wouldn't get her circus badge! She didn't want to be the only Pee Wee without a badge! How awful to have a blank spot on her shirt where the circus badge should be!

She pictured Mrs. Peters feeling sorry for her and giving her a badge anyway. A pity badge! Molly didn't want a pity badge. A badge for doing nothing. She wanted to earn her badge like everyone else! She had to be in that center ring tomorrow no matter what! And she would be. Even if she was the only one there!

And that was just about what happened. In the morning the thunder clapped and the lightning lit up the sky. Her dad yelled, "Run between the drops!"

When Molly and her parents arrived, no one was in the tent, not even Max. At least the tent is still up, thought Molly. At least the circus is still in town.

"People will come soon," said her mother. "It's early."

But it wasn't early. It was right on time. Ten o'clock.

Soon Mrs. Peters came in, dripping wet and sneezing. "Mr. Peters is home with the baby," she said. "We didn't think we should take him out on a day like this."

The five of them listened to the water pound on the canvas overhead. There was a little leak in the roof, and Molly noticed a small stream of water flowing through the center ring. She knew Fluffy did not like water. She wouldn't like it dripping on her head!

At last Max came in, and then Mary Beth.

"Where is everyone?" asked Molly's friend.

"I don't know where anybody is. Including Roger," Molly worried. "I can't do my act without Roger and Fluffy!"

At eleven o'clock, no one else had come. Molly thought any minute Mrs. Peters would say, "Let's all go home where it's nice and dry and forget this act. Molly deserves the badge for getting this far."

But she didn't say that. And neither did Molly's parents. Max looked doubtful.

"I'm afraid no one is coming," he said. "Maybe we should close up shop."

"No way!" said Jody and Kevin, bursting into the tent.

"It took my dad a long time to get here because of the mud on Main Street," said Jody. "Where is everyone else?"

Molly knew she could depend on Jody and Kevin! Both of them had fought the rain and wind and mud for her! What a problem to decide which one of them she should marry!

"Why don't we proceed with just us?" said Mrs. Peters. "Seven people is a fine crowd!"

"But I can't go on without Roger and Fluffy!" said Molly.

"Who is Fluffy?" asked Mr. Duff.

Molly couldn't answer that without revealing the surprise ending of her trick! She felt like crying. Fluffy was supposed to be pulled out of a hat, not walk in with Roger!

"I'll run over to Roger's house and get them," said Kevin, bounding out of the tent into the rain.

What a friend, thought Molly. And what a traitor Roger was! He was probably in bed right now snoring away and forgetting all about Molly's magic act.

While they waited, Mary Beth whispered, "Do your scarf act! I'll announce it!"

Molly took her soggy cape out of her bag and put it on. Her paper crown had ripped. She took the soggy wool scarf out of the bag and folded it as small as she could and stuffed it into the rubber thumb. Most of it wouldn't fit. She put the fake thumb on her real thumb. But it kept popping off. Molly was glad magic was not her real job. It would be a terrible way to earn a living.

"Ladies and gentlemen, friends and family, boys and girls of all ages," Mary Beth announced from the center ring, "I present Molly Duff, famous magician! She will now perform the world-famous magic scarf trick. Note that there is no red scarf anywhere in sight."

Molly was afraid everyone could see her scarf, but she had to go on now that Mary Beth had started the show. She walked into the center of the ring and took a big breath.

"I will now say the magic words to magically summon a red scarf. Don't blink or you'll miss it. Ready, set, ziss, boom, bah!"

At her words Kevin and Roger burst in. The small audience turned around to look at the boys at the same time that Molly tugged the scarf out of her false thumb. When the audience turned back to her, it really did look as if the scarf had appeared by magic!

"Wow!" said Jody. "That was great!"

"Thanks," Molly said, smiling.

The tent was filled with applause, as seven people clapped loudly.

Molly was excited. She had performed her first trick!

And Roger was here so her act could go on. But Molly didn't see any rabbit. Where was Fluffy?

CHAPTER 9

The Best Act of All

"Ladies and gentlemen," Molly said. "Please excuse me while I talk to my assistants." She hurried over to the Pee Wees.

"Rat's knees!" she said, stamping her foot. "Where is Fluffy?"

"Fluffy is having babies," said Roger. "She can't be in your act."

"But you promised!" cried Mary Beth.

"Well, how did I know she was going to have babies this morning?" said Roger. "It's not my fault!"

"You always say that," said Mary Beth.

But even Molly knew it would be hard to blame Roger for this. He couldn't do anything about a rabbit having babies on the day of her circus magic act.

"I've got a toy rabbit at home," said Kevin.

Kevin was always helpful.

"Just do the ventriloquist act," said Mary Beth, frowning. "That's more than enough magic to get the badge."

But Molly dreaded the ventriloquist act the most. Why was *it* the only one left? She took off her cape and followed Roger to the center ring. Max put a spotlight on her. Roger tripped over an empty pail and fell to his knees. The audience began to laugh. This is not a good start, thought Molly.

"Presenting the world-famous ventriloquist, Molly Duff," said Mary Beth. "She can throw her voice for miles and no one can see her lips move."

"Hey!" Roger shouted. "I'm the ventriloquist. She's the dummy! That was part of the deal!"

"The deal was you'd bring us a rabbit!" Mary Beth whispered loudly. "You didn't, so you have to be the dummy!"

The crowd laughed harder. They must think this is part of the act, thought Molly.

Molly sat down on a chair Max had put in the ring. She didn't know if it was better to have to sit on Roger's knee or to have Roger sit on hers. Neither one would be any fun.

"I'm not sitting on Molly Duff's lap!" screamed Roger.

"Yes, you are!" said Mary Beth, shoving him onto Molly's knee before he could get away. Roger fell over backward, and the

audience roared. Kevin was laughing loudly. Mary Beth was motioning to Molly to begin.

"How old are you, little boy?" said Molly to the dummy.

Roger had turned red. He said, "I'm seven and you know it and I'm not a little boy."

"You aren't supposed to answer!" said Mary Beth. "You're just supposed to move your lips!"

There was a noise in the back of the tent, and Sonny came in. He pointed at Roger and roared with laughter.

"Roger's got a girlfriend," he sang. "Roger's got a girlfriend."

Roger turned even brighter red and screamed, "She's not my girlfriend!"

"Hey, can the dummy sing a song?" called Sonny.

"This is good," said Mary Beth. "Audience participation! Let's hear a song, dummy!"

But how could Molly sing a song without moving her lips? A song that looked as if Roger was singing it? She tried, but nothing came out.

When Roger heard the people shout "Song! Song!" he felt a sudden urge to show off. He began to sing "Three Blind Mice." When the audience clapped, he stood up and sang more loudly. Soon the whole audience joined in. Max handed Roger a cane and he began to strut around the center ring, dancing and doing cartwheels.

The response was so great, and everyone was having such a good time, that Roger sang another song. And another. All eyes were on him!

"It's your act," said Mary Beth glumly. "I don't like how he's taking it over!"

But the audience was in stitches. It was a good act, no matter who did it.

When Roger finally stopped singing, Max grabbed the microphone. "Ladies and gentlemen, how about a hand for Molly Duff and her funny dummy, Roger?" The crowd clapped and people came up front to congratulate Roger and Molly on their comedy act.

"It isn't a comedy act," Molly said to Mary Beth. "It's a magic act."

"It's better as a comedy act," whispered Mary Beth. "Just let them think that."

Now everyone was shaking Molly's hand and Roger's hand and saying they didn't know when they'd had so much fun. Max was passing out free popcorn and everyone ate as much as they wanted. By the time Roger and Molly had finished taking their bows, the sun was out!

"Look!" said Mrs. Peters. "Your act was so good it made the storm go away!"

Max gathered the group around. "Sea Bees, thank you for your help. This was a great *two*-day circus. We've never had two shows in one town before. It was fun—and we made lots of money for charity. Now, just leave it to us to pack everything up. We'll see you the next time the circus comes to town!"

On the way home, Molly's mom said, "I had no idea you had such a big song-and-dance act planned!"

"It was the best act of all," said her dad.

Molly decided no one had to know that her comedy act was an accident and not what she had planned.

The next Tuesday meeting at Mrs. Peters's house was badge day. Roger had

Fluffy and her babies in a big cardboard box. Everyone stood in line to see them.

"Aren't they cute!" said Rachel. "They look sooo soft!"

"It's good Fluffy had these babies," said Mary Beth to Molly. "I don't think the hat act would have been as good as the one you did."

She was definitely right, thought Molly. The comedy act was a lot more fun than pulling a rabbit out of a hat. Maybe she should be a comedian when she grew up. Make people laugh. Although she was not sure she could do it on purpose. And she wouldn't want to work with Roger!

Mrs. Peters clapped her hands and everyone sat down at the table.

"I think the circus project was a big success," she said. "We helped earn lots of money for charity, and we had fun at the same time. And that's the best way of doing things. All of you worked very hard at your acts, and they were all a success. So let's pass out the new badges!"

The Pee Wees whistled and shouted and stamped on the floor. They loved new badges. Molly's worry and work were always worthwhile when she got that new badge to put on her shirt.

Mrs. Peters called out their names and handed each Pee Wee a badge with a trapeze embroidered on it in red and a little acrobat wearing blue tights.

"That's Roger!" yelled Sonny. "In those girl's tights!"

Roger got up and punched Sonny on the arm. "Take that, Sonny Stoke!" he said. "Little Sea Bee Stoke the Bloke!"

Everyone laughed and began to chant, "Sea Bees, Sea Bees, Sea Bees!"

"I think we should change our name to the Sea Bees," said Lisa. "We could wear yellow uniforms with wings on them and look like real bees."

Rachel groaned. "Dumb," she said.

"I think the Pee Wees is a great name," laughed Mrs. Peters. "You can't top the Pee Wees!"

Their leader was right, thought Molly. No matter how hard you tried, you couldn't top the Pee Wees.

"I wonder what badge we'll earn next," said Tim. "Maybe it will be a zoo badge."

"Or a camping badge," said Patty. "I like to camp out."

Whatever it was, Molly knew it would mean a good time.

The Scouts ate their cupcakes and sang their song and said their pledge. Rat's knees, Pee Wee Scouts was fun!

Pee Wee Scout Song

♪ ♪   (to the tune of   ♪ ♪
"Old MacDonald Had a Farm")

Scouts are helpers, Scouts have fun,
Pee Wee, Pee Wee Scouts!
We sing and play when work is done,
Pee Wee, Pee Wee Scouts!

With a good deed here,
And an errand there,
Here a hand, there a hand,
Everywhere a good hand.

Scouts are helpers, Scouts have fun,
Pee Wee, Pee Wee Scouts!

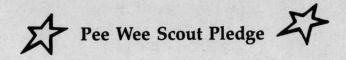

Pee Wee Scout Pledge

We love our country
And our home,
Our school and neighbors too.

As Pee Wee Scouts
We pledge our best
In everything we do.